RIDER

Harry Gamboa Jr.

D1614313

Fiction

Fiction, Photographs, Design:
All Rights Reserved
©2009, Harry Gamboa Jr.

Proofreader
Ruben Mendoza

Photograph of Harry Gamboa Jr. used with permission:
©2009, Manuel Alejandro Rodriguez

ISBN   1448670306

EAN-13   9781448670307

2009
Los Angeles

www.harrygamboajr.com

405 Freeway and Getty Center Drive

A thick layer of fog has descended onto the freeway, obscuring the path of several thousand southbound motorists, causing them to slow down as they become lost in the impenetrable opaque void of grayness.

"Hey driver, make a U-turn. I don't want to die along with these fucking losers. They make me want to puke. Pull over. I need to relieve myself immediately."

Several sleeping riders are on board the bus, others are fully awake but remain aloof and isolated in their small-screen virtual worlds of hand-held electronic devices, some are terrified by the man who is yelling as he reaches down inside the crotch of his pants.

"I'm afraid we ain't gonna make it this time. I just gotta piss."

The man unbuckles his pants and urinates against the rear door.

"You pussies make me laugh."

A young woman with a shaved head walks up to the man and quickly strikes his penis with a foot-long length of orange colored spray painted rebar. Piss and blood splatter recklessly as the man tries to catch his breath to scream. She lifts the bar again but the man punches her in the face. The fight is on.

The driver opens the rear doors of the articulated bus allowing for the man and woman to spill out and brawl in the emergency lane as the traffic begins to move again.

"Move away from the doors. I'm going to leave them open until the liquid is dry."

I look out the window from the elevated rear seat to view the belongings of motorists as they drive past: Toys, laptop computers, books, fast food, hammers, backpacks, and various items that become a blur before they can be identified. I see several deer grazing on the dry brush alongside the hills of the Sepulveda Pass.

"The man's dick fell on the floor."

I am wearing an azure colored turtleneck sweater with matching sunglasses and have taken a vow of nonviolence for the day in order to avoid direct conflict with strangers, former lovers, and avowed enemies.

2

"Don't touch it. It's made of plastic and fell out of the woman's purse during the scuffle."

The sky is now completely blackened by the mixture of diesel exhaust, smoke, and oddly formed clouds. The deer are coughing as soot fills their nostrils and eyes. The black cloud has entered the bus, filling us all with a sudden sense of dread. I pull the neon-yellow cord, triggering a recorded announcement.

"Next stop, Getty Center Drive. Thank you for riding Metro".

The bus continues moving slowly towards the off ramp.

"I've heard about women and men who use such things. They often give them names like they would their pets. It's absolutely disgusting. I will forever be a virgin. The thought of penetration and the sharing of body fluids is obscene. That's why I murdered my parents."

"I've been riding the buses since 5:00 a.m. and now it is 7:00 p.m. Maybe the smog has gotten into my brain but it sounds like you just said that you murdered your parents."

"It's not a tragedy or a complex. They deserved to die for bringing me into this world. I didn't ask to be here. I might as well be useful for something."

The young man with long fingernails produces a .45 calibre pistol from his coat pocket. He points the gun out the window and fires several shots hitting one of the deer in the hind leg. It struggles to limp away but a coyote appears from behind a tree and pounces on the deer. The dying deer is dragged away by its broken neck.

"You in the back, put that away. No shooting until we get to the inner city."

The bus driver's voice is broadcast loudly over damaged speakers.

"That wasn't very sporting of you."

"Fuck off. Maybe I'll waste another bullet."

3

R
I
D
E
R

1st Street and Main Street

I'm wearing all black today.

The temperature reached 105 degrees Fahrenheit by 8:00 a.m. Dry hot Santa Ana winds are blowing. The air conditioner is malfunctioning and is spewing acrid fumes that fill the bus. All of the windows are sealed shut.

I've kept my eyes closed for more than an hour. I took a look out the window at the blue ocean in Santa Monica then suddenly felt an unexplainable sense of exhaustion. I'm too tired to see everything. I should have gotten off the bus at La Cienega boulevard but something compels me to be thrown off the bus at the end of the line at Union Station. I'll leave everything up to chance. I've made a vow of randomness for today.

"So I was licking his face, then licking her face, but then this guy comes over like it is any of his business and tells us to mind our manners, shit, by the time we stopped beating him, he was licking our ass holes."

The girl's voice has a metallic shrill tone. It is coming from the speaker function of a digital mobile phone.

"Yeah, I like to party whenever I feel like it. Too bad I got stabbed. Some guys like it when something is missing. It adds spice, you know."

Exhaustion.

"Put it louder. Hey, anyone want to see me fuck?"

Maybe I'm imagining the monologue, not sure if I've been dreaming. I'm wondering what she might look like. The gang-infused tonality, the incredibly youthful nihilistic bravado. She must be beautiful and bent on an early suicide.

"Yeah, I want to see you fuck."

I put my hands to my face. No, it's not my mouth that moved. I haven't said anything since yesterday. I never say what I mean unless it will result in rewards or punishment.

"I want you to lick my face so that I can shoot you in the mouth."

The man's voice has a Midwestern assured threat about it. A gun is

4

©2009, Harry Gamboa Jr.

probably pointed at the mobile phone. The mouthpiece must be very
wet. But who is holding the phone?

"*Puto*, I won't let you shoot anything into my mouth."

The bell rings and the bus pulls over stopping at the curb. The door
opens briefly, allowing hot wind to blow in. The door closes. It is an
older model bus without many of the contemporary automated features
found on other lines.

The exhaustion extends beyond my body and mind. It has more to do
with the extension of boredom acquired over many decades of repeti-
tive actions, situations, thoughts, images, and words. I have this sense
of having travelled several billion miles through space. I am a human
being on the planet earth with inherited traits that link me directly to the
beginning of it all. I feel it. This is how most dreams begin.

"Is he dead?"

"He won't open his eyes."

"I'm not dead. I'm blind."

"You're not blind. I saw you get on the bus and nothing was wrong with
you.

"Everything is wrong. I wanted to see the murals of *Aztlán* but lost my
vision on Venice boulevard. The same thing happened to my father
and grandfather. One day, they each were hit with sudden blindness.
They both strangled their wives, then killed themselves. My poor
mother and grandmother never knew what hit them. Luckily, I'm single.
Where are we?"

"We? Nobody's with you, brother. You are all alone in this world."

"There was this girl, she wanted me to see her fuck."

"You've got a filthy mouth for a blind man."

"I'll never get to see her do anything."

"You've got to exit the bus. This is the last stop."

"Can you help me get to the next bus?"

"The blind can lead themselves. Now get off!"

5

Metrolink Glendale Station

No vows today. No theoretical musing. No ritualistic acts.

For nearly a decade, I rode heavy rail commuter trains to my various part-time jobs in Valencia, Riverside, Oxnard, Irvine, Lancaster,
Oceanside, and Northridge. Sometimes the jobs overlapped so that I'd
be in multiple cities on a daily or weekly basis. It became necessary to
get to Union Station by 5:50 a.m. at least four days per week. I easily became adapted to long commuting days. I always attempted to be
productive by setting myself to work on a variety of projects that could
be completed over several months while sitting at one of the few tables
on the upper level of the trains during 80 mph commutes to disparate
points of Southern California.

During the past few years, two disastrous Metrolink train wrecks occurred with each accident resulting in multiple fatalities. The most
horrific incident involved a 45 mph head-on collision with a freight train.
The Metrolink locomotive was pushed back into its first passenger car,
causing it to disintegrate like a crushed plastic toy, killing everyone
inside. In both accidents, the majority of the fatalities involved people
who had been sitting at tables.

Faulty design, missing safety features, outsourced operators, diversion
of funds, and the built-in multi levels of systematic governmental and
corporate corruption resulted in mass killings with no individuals bear-
ing any blame at all. I've avoided riding the Metrolink trains because
nothing has been changed to alter the high probabilities of another
deadly train wreck.

Today is different.

I've received a message from a dear friend who has been diagnosed
with a terrible disease. She most likely will not survive the week because she has decided against receiving any treatment that could possibly extend her life (while destroying her quality of life).

Her note:

> **You must come by quickly. Let's listen to some music
> and have a glass of wine. I must tell you a secret before
> you find out from my husband, or my ex, or my sisters.
> I know that you won't hold anything against me. And it
> isn't a confession. You already know that I aborted your
> child when we were still too young to fear the future.**

6

She was ultimately beautiful the first day I saw her. Our intimate friend-
ship came from a series of moments that now seem to be from another
time and another life altogether. I have not spoken with her for many
years and wonder why she is seeking me out in her last few days.

I am sitting facing backwards in the middle passenger car of a Metrolink
train that consists of two locomotives and three passenger cars. I am
not at a table.

"Tickets. Take out your tickets!"

A military-style uniformed police officer is accompanied by a large ag-
gressive dog that is wearing black K-9 protective armor. The officer has
a 9mm pistol on his belt holster and a .45 calibre pistol strapped to his
right leg. The effect is intimidating for anyone who should have nothing to worry about. The objective of controlling the population at large
supersedes the need to prevent destructive acts. The police should
apprehend the bureaucrats who have already killed scores of people on
similar trains.

"Your ticket is invalid."

The dog is snarling menacingly.

"Oh, sorry, this is what they call a hand-written note. I used to be in
love with her. Is this printed thing what you're looking for? Should I
show it to the dog too?

"I.D."

I pull out my wallet with more than ten picture I.D. cards from my various places of employment.

"Place your forefinger here."

The officer holds out a portable electronic device that scans my finger-
print.

"You'll receive the response-delay violation citation in the mail."

The officer and dog move on.

The train moves quickly as it sways from side to side, barely missing
the hundreds of freight cars on shared tracks. I feel like I've nearly
avoided a major collision and am now focused on the final secret that
will be revealed to me like a flickering light from a dying star.

7

Whittier Boulevard and Lorena Street

"Man, I never thought I'd see you around here again. I've heard a few things about you and thought that you'd be living the high life in Paris or Pelican Bay. Someone told me you used to drive around in a red Mercedes-Benz. You lost it all, that's all. Shit, I remember when girls were always touching your hair. That's gone too. What the fuck are you looking at? These ain't my real teeth."

Every time I cross over the L.A. River it doesn't take long for me to encounter someone from my old neighborhood of Boyle Heights. Most of the people I knew have moved elsewhere while others have never gone more than a few blocks away from where they have spent their entire lives. Some people have produced great art and have improved their social environment. A few have decided to indulge themselves in lost causes and a lesser group have simply given up.

"I remember when we were kids, man. We ditched school together. The streetcars used to pass through here. It was the R-car line on Whittier boulevard. My uncle was walking home drunk one night and got killed by the P-car on 1st Street. He was cut in half on the corner of Indiana street. His head was in the city and his ass was in the county. The guys at the mortuary wanted to charge my aunt double, those fuckers."

"Yeah, I went to the funerals, part one and part two. A week later, they caught you sniffing glue in the classroom. After that, it didn't take long for you to stick a needle in your arm."

"It was hard, man. My arms were skinnier than the needles. I was a *tecato* for more than twenty years but now I'm a vegan, *ese*. All I eat is green stuff and drink water with more green stuff. My wife says I look younger than my oldest son from my first marriage. She should know. She's been married six times already."

"I'll bet she's a smoker, drinker, and sharp thinker."

"I'm glad you brought that up, man. You've got to look them in the eye and tell them that you love them all day long but always, and I mean always, keep a lookout for the sharp things in their hands. You just never know."

"My ex missed my heart by only a few inches."

"No way man, you don't got a heart."

8

"Next stop, Lorena Street."

The automated voice has taken on a sophisticated accent, much like a learned scholar, somewhat akin to a British stage actor.

"You're going straight ahead and not getting off here? Get down here with your *gente*. Your mom lives a block from here and your dad's buried right over there. Oh, I get it. You don't want them to see you with that black eye. A girl gave it to you. That's what you get for being a lover boy. You can't change your stripes no matter which way they're pointing. See you later."

Not a black eye. Fake eyelashes. His vision must be very poor. Too much heroin, cocaine, mescaline, LSD, angel dust, crank, crud, raw alcohol, and Quaaludes. He might be eating his greens but I'm certain it won't restore his ability to discern past from present, good from bad, or sharpen his memory. The last time I saw him was when we were in our twenties, he was chasing me with a knife. I was always faster than him. I knew every inch of the barrio and had a holographic under-standing of every possible escape route from any point and in every direction. He believed a rumor that his second wife had been involved in a sexual relationship with me. It was an unsubstantiated rumor that happened to be false. He was high on multiple drugs that gave him the strength of several men but he was quite fuzzy on what was up or down. He threatened to kill me if he ever saw me again. He was like a rabid beast. He was yelling and screaming while I laughed and skipped like a mindless child. He should have known that something bad would happen. He tripped and stabbed himself in the lower abdomen. He left a trail of blood before losing consciousness and expelling his spleen. I'm glad he's alive but like he said, you just never know.

"I love your dress. Lavender chiffon is always best. Here, take this holy relic, a word from Our Savior, you already look like heaven."

Not a dress, but a vintage straight jacket that should accurately match the blooming jacaranda trees when I take my stroll along Whittier bou-levard near Salazar Park. The video will be on the Internet by tonight. I do not accept her painted plaster cross as I gaze into her dark eyes.

"I'll pray for you anyway, *viejo*. We can be good friends forever in the hereafter."

The young woman looks a bit too attractive to be concerned with the hereafter. I offer her a small disposable bottle of vodka for the here and now. She opens the cap and drinks it quickly. Maybe the spirits will move her to sing and dance with me on the streets of East L.A.

5 Freeway and Lyons Avenue

I'm on the wrong bus. I waited nearly three hours for the bus that could take me to Warner Center in the San Fernando Valley but then the sun went down. Impulsively, I ran into the busy street and frantically waved down the last bus that was headed to Century City, otherwise, I might have gotten stuck in Valencia until tomorrow morning.

"Good evening. Welcome, fellow rider."

The man in the dark colored suit looks like I've seen him on television. He's carrying a family-sized box of detergent on his lap.

"I've been selling an idea.

"Any buyers?"

"I have no idea. You see, it's my face and voice. I was born to be an advertising image and spokesperson. I can tell you to buy so-and-so detergent and a viable percentage of viewers will switch brand loyalty as they head off to the nearest laundromat. I can increase the smoking habit in any target market simply by putting a cigarette to my lips, taking a puff, then giving a big broad smile of satisfaction. I can make you agree to give away your money freely, convince you to borrow money at high interest rates, but most importantly, encourage you to continue working so that you'll have more money to participate in an endless cycle of blatant exploitation. It's a wonderful and easy profession."

I've been up since 4:00 a.m. and have put in a full day at work. I'm lucky to have any job at all. The new economic reality has me work-ing harder, longer hours, and in more places for less gross income. I was born to have fun but learned much later in life that my social role is closer to that of a seemingly tireless worker ant.

"Are you the guy who introduced the world to everything that is cleaner, brighter, and whiter?"

"It is all about hypnotic effects and group gullibility. All passive view-ers are my very best friends. I've whitewashed so many minds that it makes my head spin. I'm the generic version of what you are most familiar with in terms of advertising campaigns. My ego is in check and I'm quite frugal as you can see. A one-way ticket costs only $4.00 for a comfortable commuter ride aboard this bus. That comes out to .10¢ per mile times forty. There, you see, I'm trying to sell you on the idea even though you are already on board."

"I must admit that you are quite persuasive even in real life. I wonder if you could talk the driver into a spontaneous re-routing of our trajectory so that I could be dropped off at Warner Center before you get to Avenue of the Stars. That would add an extra 40 miles to your trip and double your savings by costing you only .05¢ per mile".

"That's an excellent idea. I'm sure he won't be able to resist."

There are several commuter bus systems that offer morning and evening service between the desert regions and urban areas, the beaches and various valley communities, outlying suburbia and the corporate centers in Orange County, Ventura County, as well as the Inland Empire. The buses are similar to tour buses with cushioned seats and other amenities that provide full comfort during the long haul. Each workweek morning, commuter buses bring uniquely trained and upper level employees, as well as police officers, from the surrounding areas into the central city so that they can then function in their specified roles. At the end of the day they can all board the buses back to the relative safety of their communities leaving the city and its residents behind without ever looking back. I utilize the commuter buses in the inverse pattern and spend many of my days in their neighborhoods while they are away and then leave before they get back.

"The driver says he'll do it if someone treats him to a drive-thru takeout order of a cheeseburger, fries, and a soft drink. I'd also like to have a strawberry shake as my 10% of the deal. What do say?"

"That's stupendous. You really are amazing. Tell him there's a great place on Tampa boulevard off of the 118 freeway. Their burgers smell so good that they attract cougars that come in from the hills. The unpaved parking lot has been the scene of several fatal attacks on wild animals and unruly customers by the restless armed guards who truly believe that there is no such thing as a free lunch.

"Wild burgers, he'll like that".

All of the interior lights have been switched off. We are shadows in the darkness. The speeding headlights of oncoming traffic pass in an endless stream of unconsciousness. The air conditioned bus glides smoothly along the 5, 405, and 118 freeways as the landscape changes from the sparsely populated hills of Santa Clarita to the epicentral area of many quakes that have jolted the San Fernando Valley.

"Next time I see you on TV, I'll be sure to change the channel."

The man in the suit never says another word.

11

Sunset Boulevard and Westerly Terrace

When I was a young boy in the middle of the 20th Century, I often ran happily and playfully on the sidewalk along Sunset boulevard near the front of my home in the Silverlake District. I was usually grinning mischievously because of an inherent optimism that all would be fun and games in my life. My parents were young during that era.

"Fucking dumb bitch. Gimme your money."

The drug addict has a gun pointed at a woman.

"All of you gonna give me your money."

The bus is filled with workers, students, elderly people, and a few others who are out to enjoy the scenery of the famed boulevard.

He turns and puts the barrel of the gun to an infant's head.

"Gonna kill the, ugh, ugly baby."

The baby senses death and screeches loud enough to hurt my ears.

"And I don't care who says shit cuz you all nothin' but sad fucks anyways."

A worker with gardening sheers moves quickly, lopping off the young man's hand as it clutches the pistol.

"Mauhcatlayecoani."

A homeless woman immediately picks up the severed hand and places it into a large green plastic bag that is filled with a diverse collection of undervalued and worthless urban detritus.

The baby's mute mother retrieves the pistol from the floor and puts it into a diaper bag.

The addict has nearly fainted in shock as two university students use his ripped shirt as a makeshift tourniquet. Another student comes forth and places a folded pink towel into his mouth to ensure his silence.

"We'll get him to the hospital on Vermont. Here, take our picture with my phone. I'll get extra credit when I write my thesis paper: **Street Justice, Mayhem, and Neo-Capitalism in Post-American Society**."

12

The bus continues to move forward as though nothing out of the ordi-
nary has just taken place. It is an inner city model that is designed for
constant stop-and-go action. These types of buses are each fitted with
two flat screen monitors near the front and rear doors to provide endless propaganda video clips in English and Spanish that promote the
elevation of the lowest forms of popular culture. The audio is usually
set to high volume. Every few minutes text-based pop quizzes will appear on screen asking trivial questions that elementary school dropouts
would find easy to answer but that somehow insinuate a subliminal
message that real life has no value at all. Much of the content pro-
motes military recruitment with the focus mostly directed to the financial
gain that could be made by participating in the fun aspects of military
service. There is no hint of warfare. There is no mention of violence.
The video clips provide a utopian world of hyperactive beautiful young
people who are flying, running, smiling, and looking like they have a
secured bright future that is superior in all ways to anything that the bus
riders could ever have unless they join today.

"They should give him an overdose of whatever he's already on, dump
him near the subway station, and let nature do the rest."

"Human nature does it best."

"Hey, look at that. The hand's still moving in the bag."

Some of the passengers comment endlessly while others look on with
a silent wariness of already having seen similar situations escalate into
dangerously worse circumstances.

The gentrification of the Silverlake neighborhood has proven to serve
as a buffer against the worsening economic conditions that have overtaken many parts of Los Angeles. My connection to this area goes
back to when my mother and father would take me for a ride on the
Pacific Electric Railway's Red Cars down this same boulevard. I don't
believe that there were any impromptu amputations, nor incessant propaganda, or that any spoken language other than English would have
been tolerated aboard those urban trains of that era.

"Hi, I was jobless and school didn't matter much to me. My parents
were disappointed in me. I thought it was all over at such an early age
but then I found out about how I could serve my country in the company
of the best people you could ever know. Now I'm making good money,
I've seen the world, I have good friends who are always there to back
me up, and most important of all, my parents are proud of me. Contact
your local recruiter so that you can have a great life like me. If I can do
it, anyone can."

13

Metro Rail Red Line Universal City Station

The subway system of Los Angeles consists of a lackluster series of trains that move back and forth along a forked path with each branch ending at uncompleted tunnels, leaving riders somewhat shortchanged at incongruous locations in the Mid-Wilshire District of Los Angeles and at the Noho District in the San Fernando Valley. Each of the several subterranean stations are poorly lit, minimally ventilated, and decorated with committee-approved public art. The return trip from each route leads to an unceremonious drop-off at Union Station, which is located across the street from the famed tourist destination of Olvera Street, and within walking distance of the nefarious Twin Towers Los Angeles County Detention Facility,

"Stand clear, the doors are closing."

It is a shrill command voiced by beta-version software.

I have completed three hours of work at one job in Chatsworth and am now off for an additional two hours of work in South Pasadena. I'll ride more than 80 miles via trains and buses today. I'll return to the Venice area tonight, only to get six hours of sleep before the next day that will play out to a different workday schedule.

I have maintained a vow of public transportation silence today. If any-one talks to me, under any and all circumstances, I will not speak.

"This is the part of the subway that I hate. We dive nearly five miles deep and travel at 90 mph until we go completely under and beyond the Hollywood Hills. They say that if there is ever a deadly earthquake, or terrorist bomb, or poison gas, that we'll all be executed by the secret police. I've already vomited a few times just thinking about this. It is bad enough that every time I stand on the platform all I can think about is how all of my problems would be solved if I jumped onto the electri-fied third rail. What's wrong with you? Ain't you got no empathy?"

The man moves away to the other end of the rail car leaving a stagnant stench of partially decayed human remains.

"Hey, Mr. Feces, we're giving you a bath before this thing is over."

Three teenaged boys are donning red velvet berets. One of the boys is wearing a yellow rain coat that he pulls back revealing a pressurized hose nozzle. He turns the lever and a powerful stream of water strikes the foul-smelling man in the face. Another boy rushes over to him and

14

pours nearly a quart of green viscous fluid detergent onto his head. The third boy produces an industrial strength scrub brush that has been fitted to the end of a stainless steel rod. The man's futile attempt to ward off the unexpected cleansing is accompanied by moans and gasps that would normally be associated with drowning. The scrubbing and spraying action is furiously effective and within a few minutes the rail car is overcome with a fresh wintergreen scent.

"Stand clear, the doors are opening."

The water pours out through the open doors and the teenaged boys have already exited quickly disappearing beyond view of the train. The man is sobbing and staring at me with a hateful glare but says nothing.

"Stand clear, the doors are closing."

Time appears to be suspended as the train travels through the concrete-lined tunnel. I'm feeling a bit dizzy. It could be the onset of a virus or simply another bout of exhaustion. Maybe it is motion sickness. I close my eyes and suddenly fall deeply into a micro-sleep.

The dream takes the form of a distorted memory, in which I am holding my son's hand when he is only 4-years old. He is excited about his new toy. It is a big gray machine-gun. He is pointing it at colorful balloons in the sky and shoots every circular target with deadly panache. I'm about to take the gun away from him when I find myself holding my daughter's hand when she is also 4-years old. She is telling me a complicated tale about the tormented souls of children who were tortured and murdered in jails during an immigration sweep. She takes a crayon and makes an abstract drawing of the written language by which the souls relay their desire to return to their rightful place among the living. The drawing looks very much like the gang-styled cryptic graffiti that can be found on nearly every type of urban surface.

"Stand clear, the doors are opening."

The man has regained his composure and now looks like a world-class citizen. He has abandoned all of his belongings consisting of plastic bags, piles of cardboard, and a torn blanket. He is smiling confidently and waves as he exits the train.

"Stand clear, the doors are closing."

I close my eyes and slip into unconsciousness. In the continuing dream, my children are sitting happily next to me. It has become a peaceful and reassuring dream that will last only until the final stop.

15

Huntington Drive and Story Place

"So, if you've got a minute, I'll tell you, but that's only if it isn't any both-er. First off, I've never met the woman. She never put her lips on me and I can't imagine touching her without her consent. She's lying. She just wants to cause trouble. She's always been a liar. She's always a bitch. She tells everyone she ever meets that we are lovers. There are pictures of her everywhere on the Internet but I've never seen her in real life. She's used some kind of picture software to make it look like we're having sex, like we're enjoying a picnic, like we're dancing at a club. Just look at me, I'm so fucking ugly, so disfigured, so deformed, and she's so beautiful. Why would she do this to me? It's all about her sick game of degrading me in public. If I ever do see her, I'll kill her. She tells everyone that I enjoy doing perverted things to her and that I let her do the same things to me. I've never used a dildo. I was raised Catholic and shouldn't even think about it. I can't take it anymore. There is such a thing as justifiable homicide. I've been told that she lives in one of these upper class homes in San Marino. She'll have the surprise of her life when I finally get to confront her."

A man with a shaky hand is sketching a picture of me. He doesn't real-ize that I can see what he's doing because I avert my eyes every time he looks away from his drawing pad. He's drawn an accurate depiction of who I might be in an idealized world. I'm not sure what he intends to do with the picture but I'm not in the mood to strike up a conversation related to art theory. The other man speaks loudly into his two-fisted Blackberry and iPhone.

"Yeah, that's it. Kill her."

The artist should be making a detailed drawing of the man who is mak-ing the verbal threats. It could prove to be an invaluable tool for the police in catching him should he carry out his intended crime.

"The worst part about it, and I know you might think that I'm crazy for saying so, is that I'm falling in love with her. No one has ever paid any attention to me. Like I said, I don't know what her lips taste like. No way man, I don't want to see her tits."

There are some people who are completely uninhibited when talk-ing on a mobile phone. They yell, grimace, throw kisses, gesticulate with strange hand combinations that attempt to convey meaning to the listener on the receiving end, spit, cry, or talk loud enough so that ev-eryone riding on a moving bus can hear their entire conversation. I've seen some people throw punches into the air or stomp on the ground when talking on mobile phones.

16

"Hey, driver, I'm getting off at the next stop. I've got a heavy load, so get me close to the curb."

The bus pulls to a stop at the corner and operates a pneumatic device that releases compressed air allowing for the bus to tilt and be lowered until the base of the bus touches the elevated edge of the curbed side-walk. Buses with the capacity to perform such a "kneeling" function are often overly represented by nearly incapacitated riders.

"I've got to hang up now. Just watch the TV news. It'll be the bloodiest shit you've ever seen."

The man struggles to get up from his seat with the use of a reinforced aluminum-framed walker. He moves slowly and deliberately as he drags his enormous belly along the floor of the bus.

"What are you looking at fucker? This big tumor is my best buddy. The girls go wild over it. Just can't stay away. It wiggles when it doesn't cause me too much pain. If you can't stand the sight of me just look the other way. Don't stare or you'll grow one the same size up your ass."

I feel like sticking my foot out to trip him but I've made a vow to avoid physical contact with human beings, plants, and animals for the entire day.

"There is no such thing as mercy."

The man makes a clean sweep of the floor as the tumor is dragged along ominously between his legs. The artist crouches down and quickly crawls up to the rear end of the man's tumor using a brush to paint on a cartoon image of a stick of TNT and a lit fuse with some finely formed letters that spell out, "**Blow Me**". The artist returns to his seat unnoticed by the man who has become a living canvas.

"Someone stretched this bus. I don't remember it being such a long trip to the door. I'm in love, everybody. She loves me and I'm not worthy of the honor. That's why she's gonna get it."

The man finally exits the bus as the driver reverses the "kneeling" process. The bus continues moving forward as the artist returns to his work of sketching my picture. In the sketch, I'm made to look like a *Dia de Los Muertos* celebrant. I am rejuvenated in many ways. His pen perfectly captures my wine-colored wig, fine blue suit, and empty brief-case. My stop was more than a mile back. I'll remain on this bus until he's exited so that he won't be able to sneak up on me to paint a bril-liant image where it doesn't belong.

17

Mills Avenue and Baseline Road

I've decided to photograph thirty walls in Southern California that block major landmarks or celebrated points of interest. It is important that the walls be relatively close in proximity to the object or site that is being effectively obstructed from view. I have already photographed walls that have obscured Disneyland, the Hollywood Sign, Our Lady of the Angels Cathedral, all of Century City, several weapons development corporations in El Segundo, the former site of the Silver Dollar Bar in East L.A., the 10 freeway to 405 freeway exchange, MOCA, and USC. I will also include walls that blot out the views of natural wonders. The recent cold weather has created the perfect white cap on Mount Baldy that overlooks Claremont and that can be seen from most of the Los Angeles basin. I intend to display the images in an Internet solo exhibition that will be titled, **There's Nothing To See**. Each image will be a close-up of the selected wall and titled with the name of the object or site that will not be seen by the viewer.

"Way up there is where the UFO landed back in 1984. I saw it with my own eyes. That's why I was abducted. The aliens took me away for ten years but brought me back a minute before they picked me up. You can blame Einstein for that. My watch hasn't worked properly since that day but it does keep on ticking. It is no wonder why I went completely infertile the next time I made love to my ex-husband. What time is it? The bus is running late."

I've moved away from the seat next to the woman. She has a constellation of open sores on her legs. I look up to read the advertisement posters that are displayed above the seats along the length of the bus.

Research Subjects Needed
Do you have problems concentrating?
Does your skin itch?
Do you have unnatural sex?
Thoughts of suicide or homicide?
Would you like to earn $9.00 per hour?
Free parking.
Not responsible for any and all adverse events.
Sign up now!

Bus fares changing.
Coins and bills to be replaced by TAP card.
No discounts.
Monthly fare only.
Buy your TAP card at any liquor store.

18

Money for school.
Shoes for the baby.
Make your payments on time.
Join the National Guard.

$20.00 tooth extraction.
Single x-ray.
One shot of Novocaine.
5 minutes in the dentist chair.
Smile!

Tech School Is For You.
If you can read this, you qualify.
Become a professional expert in your spare time.
Fill out our E-Z loan application over the phone.
Take cap and gown photos in just a few short weeks.

Unsure of the new neighbors?
Want them to stay on their side of the fence?
Need to eliminate nagging doubt?
Frequent your local gun dealer.

The smell of camphor suddenly fills the bus as the woman lifts and swings her arms towards outer space as she reenacts her extraterrestrial exploits.

"They penetrated me in orifices that have since been sealed shut. Their slimy paws were all over me. Their green tongues are too adventuresome for my taste. I was raped in the heavens between Orion and several unknown dimensions. Ever have your skirt blown off by a comet's tail? I have seen more than you could ever imagine."

Mount Baldy is now clearly within view. I'll be using several walls from one of the nearby affluent gated communities to create the photograph that will one day hang on a computer screen.

"You are the one who is truly ignorant of the beauty and horror that fills our internal and external universes. I am you and you are nothing."

The woman has sunk quickly into a blank pause. She has become limp and stares into empty space. She looks like a sculpture that has been partially eroded by the elements.

I never photograph unattended children, unconscious people, the dead, or those who have suffered great physical and mental trauma. All of my walls are pre-existing perceptual barriers that allow me to enjoy the day.

19

Metro Rail Green Line El Segundo Station

The Metro Green Line light rail trains pass quickly alongside a parallel path next to the 105 freeway between Norwalk and Redondo Beach. The tracks are elevated and do not intersect with street traffic or cross other train tracks. It is often referred to as the train that starts at nowhere only to take you nowhere. The busiest stop is at the Rosa Parks Station where people can transfer to the Metro Blue Line that connects downtown Los Angeles to downtown Long Beach. It is a particularly busy station that is designed very much like a prison yard where hundreds of people can stand shoulder-to-shoulder with other people who should never be encountered in an enclosed space. Some of the Metro Green Line stations near LAX are placed behind unremarkable large corporate buildings that employ people who plan and design war weapons to effectively kill entire populations throughout the world. The tracks inexplicably swerve to/from the South Bay area away from the busy international airport. The multimillion dollar rail line mostly serves a swath of underdeveloped neighborhoods that offer little incentive to visit their mini-malls via public transportation.

"The guy cut me before I got on. I'm not sure what he used. Tried to pick my pocket but I pushed his wrist as soon as he punctured me. It was so crowded at the station that I couldn't see his determined hand. Maybe a knife but probably something he picked up off the street. A nail, a piece of glass, anything. I'm lucky that I moved out of the way and that someone tripped him during the crush to catch this train. I still have my wallet. I've just never fought back in my life. Up until now, everything has always gone smoothly."

The man is holding the folded pages of a newspaper to his neck. The gash isn't very deep but it is long. He seems to have put a stop to the bleeding.

"Luckily, I won't be late for work. I've got an extra shirt and tie there, and once I get washed up in the lavatory no one will know the difference. Appearances are everything. Fear is an important survival instinct but one should never reveal it to a deadly opponent. I feel that is why he didn't stab me as deeply as he could have. I looked into his eyes as though I would enjoy dying as long as I could take him with me. That's when he showed fear in his eyes. From now on, I'll carry two guns with me. One to shoot and kill. The other, only to maim."

The black headlines have been transferred in reverse onto his neck:

woL emiT llA tA ecnedifnoC remusnoC

"Better to be in one piece than to achieve peace at the loss of one's daily objective."

The train pulls to a stop. The doors open to an empty station platform. He exits without looking back. He walks directly to the rear entrance of a nondescript building with faux windows. The doors close and the train moves towards the last few stops.

"Hey, that man left his wallet on the seat."

A young couple who have been sharing earphones while listening to music on an iPod since they boarded the train in Norwalk have suddenly become animated as they take the wallet into their hands.

"Let's take a look through it to make sure he gets it in the mail. Hey, this isn't his. There's a picture of a girl on the driver's license. Take a look at all of the pretty credit cards. Shit, there's blood on it. He stole it."

"Just wipe it off. Let's go shopping."

"Hey, mister. Finders keepers. Losers weepers."

"Don't stare so hard at us or you'll get hard up."

They kiss and grope each other as she pulls at his pants and he pulls at her blouse. The inept awkwardness of their hands and the feigned narcissism produces a slight sense of revulsion in me. Maybe it's her lack of daring that announces her inadequate sexual performance or possibly it is his inability to really turn her on. Maybe they are on drugs or are simply bored with each other. He's limp and she hardly looks damp.

The train pulls to a stop. The doors open to a brightly lit station platform. The young couple stumble off the train carrying the bloody wallet. The doors close and the train moves forward.

The young couple forgot to take their iPod with them. I pick it up and wear the earphones to hear a rock song with an accelerated low-pitched psycho-sexual beat:

> **Leave it there so it can explode,**
> **I don't care if you can't write home,**
> **Just bite and don't say, whatever, or you'll lose time,**
> **Leave it there where it can blast a hole,**
> **Let it blow away the busy people.**

21

Pacific Coast Highway and Vermont Avenue

"No need to rush. They're both dead. Underneath the bus. Jaywalkers never saw what hit them. Supervisor already on the way. Cops not here yet. Yeah, I vomited. What the hell. There goes my twenty-year perfect driving record. No. I'll be late for dinner. Just leave the meatloaf on the table. Gotta go."

The driver is smoking a cigarette as he runs in and out of the bus. I can see him through the window as he bends over to look at the mangled victims while he's pulling on his hair and slapping his own face. He's already vomited several times.

"They're both wearing flannel pajamas. Goddammit, it's midday."

Some of the riders have exited the bus to gawk and take pictures. A middle-aged man rushes towards the front of the bus to steal the driver's numbered uniform jacket before running out to the street and beyond the crowd of onlookers.

"Hail Mary full of grace... Would you care to join us in praying for the souls of the unfortunate couple? It is the only right thing to do."

"I've heard of double-sleep walking before. Rare phenomenon. I'll light a candle."

Several women and men are on their knees in the center aisle, each praying in their respective native languages: Spanish, Korean, English, Nahuatl, French, Tarascan, and Vietnamese. The prayer session is performed with burning incense, rosaries, sugar skulls, and small brass bells.

"Pray for us sinners... Please, participate."

"Too many sins to help the dead."

A woman wearing indigenous Mexican clothing and Swedish-blonde braids hands me a slice of *pan de muerto* that she's retrieved from a biodegradable paper bag. A young tattooed man in dreadlocks offers everyone small plastic cups of instant Turkish coffee. A hairless boy hands me a cellophane-wrapped chocolate candy.

The bus driver clutches his gut as he lights another cigarette.

"I honked, but you two wouldn't listen."

22

Emergency vehicles with blaring sirens are approaching quickly. The crowd has grown into an unmanageable and increasingly hostile mob. The cigarette is dangling from the tip of the driver's mouth.

"Fucker killed them. Probably speeding. Bus driver thinks he's all that, but he's just a fucking murderer."

The driver vomits blood and bile.

"Devil's plague!"

Everyone panics as they move away from the driver.

"On earth as it is in heaven... I will pray for you too."

The sweet bread is flavored with cinnamon and anise. The bittersweet dark chocolate melts in my mouth as the acidic coffee flows down my throat. The feast reminds me of my childhood when I would miss elementary school to spend a day at the kitchen table listening to my aunts, uncles, and mother tell stories about their lives as they laughed, while my father, who had a completely different set of life experiences, was working in a factory only a few miles away in the industrial city of Vernon. My uncles bragged about how they killed Nazi soldiers during fierce battles in Europe and about the absurdly violent acts that they would perform while fighting in the streets of El Paso. My aunts and mother would talk about the poverty and repression that they had faced in their hometown, and the need to fulfill their lives in Los Angeles. Most of them would smoke cigarettes and none of them ever drank alcohol during daylight hours. My mother would buy *pan dulce* from local Mexican *panaderias* and *babka* from the Jewish bakeries on Brooklyn Avenue. The percolated coffee and Mexican chocolate was always hot. Such memorable days with loved ones made my early years enjoyable.

"This bus is out of service. You've got one minute to disperse. Now get off."

A police officer enters through the front door and fires a weapon at the group of worshippers, striking a woman in the cheek with a single Taser dart. Two more darts pierce her torso. A second officer walks up and engages an electric stun gun to her breast. She is convulsing in full cardiac arrest. Smoke rises from her hair, arms, and face. She bursts into white flames in a provoked case of human spontaneous combustion. She runs out through the front door, collapses on the asphalt, and is fully cremated by the intense inferno. The riders pray softly as they escape through the rear door. I am the last to leave, taking another piece of bread in memory of the tazed woman and my late relatives.

23

Broadway and 7th Street

"You must pay $30.00 in total. Six individual day passes on separate TAP cards. Same rate for adults and children. Maybe you shouldn't have had so many kids at a such a tender age."

"I'm an absolutely responsible mother. Here's the money. I don't think that I'll have to pay extra for your opinion."

"Lady, I just do my job."

I've made an oath, for today, to avoid being dragged into any kind of conflict. A recent chance encounter with an enemy turned out badly. My black suit and tie gives me an unusual sense of confidence. My white shirt is starched and pressed. My back is bleeding slightly from several unhealed knife-slash wounds. The blood stains are hidden from view and the pain is nearly gone.

"Mom, I can't stand it. I've got a million of them! They won't get off. They're crawling inside of my head."

"Shhh. Sweetheart, you're embarrassing your brothers, sisters, and me. Sit still and swallow these little purple pills."

"I'm itching all over."

"Excuse me. What that boy needs is an ass kicking. I'd be more than happy to flog him like a father ought to do. A beautiful woman like you shouldn't be riding the bus anyway."

"Thank you. He'll calm down in a minute. I've given him an extra dose of his medication."

The two younger boys look upset that their older brother is seeking and getting so much attention while two petite girls are giggling quietly.

"If he were my son, I'd turn him black and blue with my belt."

"There's no need for violence. It only generates fear, and fear results in hate. A Swiss psychiatrist is currently treating his patients with LSD to combat fear. Now that personal use of LSD and heroin is legal in Mexico City, it is no problem filling his prescription at the 24-hour pharmacies in Tijuana."

"Mom, who put the rainbow inside the bus? You're melting."

24

The woman is stunningly beautiful and so are her children. They all appear to be too beautiful. Their manner of dress is of such an affluent and stylish fashion. Their skin appears to be made of a beige-toned porcelain. Their eyes look like polished crystals. Their hair flows smoothly with such unimaginable sheen.

"I'm also a very pragmatic single mother who must fend for her children."

"Mommy, can we have some candy? We want to get high."

"Now, children. The red pills are for virility. The orange pills are for extra energy. The yellow pills are for dreaming. The pink pills take away the nervous feeling. And, they are all for sale."

"If it isn't much of a problem, I'd like to buy some of the red pills.

"That will be $25.00 for three pills."

"I'll take ten reds and four yellows."

Within a few minutes, several hundred dollars have been exchanged on board the bus for good quality narcotics and hallucinogenic drugs. The oldest boy isn't scratching his head anymore. The two little girls have laughed themselves to sleep. The other two boys are pinching each other.

I have been avoiding eye contact. The woman approaches me.

"I've seen you before, somewhere. Here's my phone number and address. I'd like you to come over for dinner tonight. Something light with white wine. Stop by at 7:30 p.m. sharp. You won't regret my offer to treat you like you've never experienced a woman in your life."

"*Encantado.*"

I take the business card and place it into my coat pocket.

"Here. This one is on the house."

She puts a purple pill to my lips as I pretend to swallow.

"Mom, a dragon and a fairy are kissing me in the ear."

She and her children soon exit the bus. I spit out the pill and tear up the card. Beautiful children are born of such sweet honey traps.

25

Metro Rail Gold Line Lake Station

The daily temperature has been consistently above 108 degrees Fahrenheit for more than a week. The air is filled with industrial soot and dirty smoke from the major fires that are raging across the barrier mountains that line the Los Angeles basin. Several thousand acres of thick brush on steep terrain are being consumed by bright orange flames. Black, gray, and white clouds of smoke give the impression that a volcano is erupting or that a nuclear bomb has exploded in the distance. The toxic mix of burning flora, fauna, and structures is an annual breathing ritual for most people who live in Southern California.

"My lungs hurt."

"Lung, dear. Singular lung."

"Oh, yes. I forgot. So many years of filtered cigarettes. Nasty habit."

"South Pasadena has certainly changed since I first arrived here from the Fatherland after the great war to work at JPL. I never thought that America could be any different than what I saw here."

"Nostalgia is a curse. It sweetens bitter memories to a fondness just short of absolution. Our golden years are a cruel blessing."

"You will always be my Rose Queen."

"And I will always salute you. *Sieg Heil*."

I've been riding the Metro Gold Line for most of the day and have scheduled meetings with several people along the designer route at various nearby coffee shops. Each meeting will affect the outcome of my next performance project as ideas, concepts, and actions are shared over cups of espresso.

"Put off that cigarette, you old bitch."

"Peasant. My Luger will teach you a lesson."

"Put it back in your coat pocket, my dearest.   Young man, it is only a harmless squirt gun. I shall extinguish the cigarette immediately."

"Dear, he is less than a dog, subhuman, and should be exterminated."

"The law of the land gives dogs more rights than he has, dearest."

"Smoking is bad for your health and so are squirt guns. Never know who might want to smoke you both with a few bullets into your wrinkly heads."

The interior of the train and all riders are coated in light gray ash. It is nearly impossible to distinguish one person from the other. Most people have their eyes closed because of the caustic effects of the smoke. Some of the chemicals in the ash interact with skin to produce an acid that burns and accelerates the aging process.

"Dear, we have lived a long wondrous life and it would be glorious to end it on a high note by eliminating the world of such a low creature."

"But your speech at Caltech will ensure your legacy, my dearest. We'll be there in less than an hour. This was supposed to be our sacred journey into the future."

"You are always correct, my queen. My vision has become clouded by old desires. It will be best to unleash my unequivocal theories on nano-technologically-induced microbe migration for DNA cleansing to ensure global social order at the appropriate venue of supreme intellectual prowess. My loyalty to purity remains unchanged."

There is a long stretch between Pasadena and Sierra Madre where the train travels along the surface level of the 210 freeway where cars and trucks frequently travel at more than 85 mph. A short concrete wall separates the speeding vehicles from the passenger section of the light rail cars.   A panoramic view through the glass and acrylic windows reveal the fragility of man-made objects when they are confronted by natural forces as the fires approach the multiple communication towers atop Mount Wilson. Los Angeles County would lose television, radio, and microwave capabilities should the towers be lost.

"Stand clear, the doors are opening."

The elderly couple step off of the train and onto the station platform. The fast moving two-way traffic causes great swirls of dust to form as they walk slowly towards the public elevator. Lost hubcaps fly past them like stray fiery meteors.

"Stand clear, the doors are closing."

"Breathe easy, once the smoke clears, the governor will rake us over the coals to pay for this massive Bar-B-Q party and present us all with an expensive and unsightly charred California bear burger. I won't eat it. The revolution will not be marinated."

27

El Monte Busway

The El Monte Busway was created nearly four decades ago in an attempt to modernize bus service by offering a speedy two-way trip on the uninterrupted paved roadway alongside the 10 freeway from the San Gabriel Valley to downtown Los Angeles. The two station stops at L.A. County Hospital/USC Medical Center and at CSULA provide convenient access to public transportation for students, patients, faculty, and medical workers. Buses continuously race along the straight and narrow corridor from early morning until late at night.

"They cancelled most of my classes, laid off some professors, and raised my fees. I'm going to change my major because recent graduates haven't had any luck in finding jobs in the field. Military recruiters are sounding better to me all the time. I've already agreed to meeting with them at my home next week."

"They call it a four-year school but looks like it'll take me seven years to graduate. I'll be priced out before I ever get to be a senior."

"I'm not sure if I could pull the trigger on the enemy if I were to become a soldier."

"I'm almost ready to go on a shooting spree at the university, in the classroom, or on the bus. There has just got to be an easy way to eliminate frustration."

"They say that they'll help me pay for college but first I'll have to fight."

Every time I ride along the busway, I look for my former home on the hillside of what is known as Metro, a neighborhood that sits directly across the freeway from City Terrace. It is a 4-bedroom house with a large elevated deck that overlooks a 10,000 square foot backyard. I lived there three decades ago when I was a young man, under a completely different set of circumstances, during a time when I was somewhat reckless with other people's feelings causing a fateful chain-reaction of personal upheaval and irreversible mistakes.

"I'm the first member of my family to go to college. My father never read a book and my mother dropped out in the 5th grade. My older brother is in prison and my two uneducated sisters are married to penniless pricks . I don't want to end up like any of them."

"I don't like the sight of blood but maybe I'll kill a thousand people with a machine gun and get a medal."

28

"You should read a thousand books Wars only make other people rich."

"I don't have much choice. I'm already too poor, with no skills, I don't want to work at low wages, I don't want to be a prostitute, and I can't imagine selling drugs."

I gave away the house to someone special with my signature on a quit claim deed. It took only a few moments. It was a minimal price to pay for my series of playful acts that were viewed by family and peers as indelible marital crimes that would never be forgotten. I had no real attachment to the house because I never unpacked my bags from the day that I moved in and ultimately walked away without them. I imagine that the bags could still be in the closet, unopened, containing nothing of value. The house was immediately sold and then subsequently resold several times at inflated prices during the economic boom times.

"Thirty class sessions in a semester and the professor is required to be furloughed nine days, meaning that we students are being cheated out of almost a third of our scheduled education. Today is a furlough day, so I've got nothing to do."

"Yeah, I'm supposed to have three class sessions today but two professors won't be on campus. The present sucks. My past was boring. I'm going to burn my books. Fuck everything."

"They're making sure that we won't have a future."

"I need to give my life some meaning. I want to prove myself in battle. You know, kill or be killed. Doesn't matter if it's in L.A., Iraq, or Afghanistan."

"But we're not warriors. Let's go to the library."

"Maybe we should fight for our right to an education."

"I've got tons of homework. We'll have to teach ourselves."

"Let's promise to buy some guns and ammo with our student loans."

The house appears briefly through the bus windows. It is painted white. I'll always remember it being a dull yellow as it nearly burned down when life was completely chaotic, intoxicating, and exciting. No one was hurt in the fire but the tension, anxiety, and destructive patterns of behavior would soon knock the house off its foundation of purpose, and push me out onto the streets. The house is no longer within sight but its black afterimage will tease me all the way to El Monte.

Pico Boulevard and Westwood Boulevard

"The radio just announced that several hundred people have been killed in coordinated attacks across the city. The 405, 10, and 101 freeways have been shut down. Traffic is backed up on all major surface streets."

"The driver is always joking around. He's a complete jackass."

"But the traffic, it hasn't moved an inch in more than an hour."

"It's the work of terrorists who have seized upon an effective idea of using automatic weapons to shoot at motorists from freeway overpasses along key vantage points where the kill ratio could be maximized."

"The driver is a fool. He makes a mockery of our society. He should be beaten into silence."

"It's a felony to harm public transportation operators while they are in the process of performing their duties."

The driver is speaking into the microphone that carries his voice through the public address system aboard the bus. His portable radio is set to a frequency that produces static noises of hisses, hums, squeaks, and vibrating whistles. The volume is at a low decibel.

"Security officials will enforce a strict curfew and anyone found to be outdoors during that time will be shot on sight."

"He's always trying to scare the riders with his fantastic tales of murder and destruction. He hates his job. He's losing his mind."

"He should quit, or they should fire him."

"There are also reports of explosions and fires in many of the major hospitals and police stations. It is more like a civil war than an isolated rebellion by dissidents. We've all been ordered to defend our way of life."

"The driver is completely mad."

"The military is on its way to combat all resistance. They will be using white phosphorus bombs and irradiated bullets to get the job done."

"He's insane, but he always gets me to my destination on time."

The interior of the new model bus is illuminated by energy-saving fluorescent lights that eliminate all shadows and produce a bluish glow on all skin surfaces. The lighting also causes teeth, whites of the eyes, and some fabrics to glow like highly radioactive fallout. Some riders resemble monstrous creatures from low-budget TV show reruns while others look more like cheerful characters from popular animated cartoon series. I can see my own reflection in the window and am amused by the artificial aura that momentarily imposes a false face of invincibility. Looking out through the window at a colorless mundane world, I can see that people are walking along the sidewalks, dining in small cafes, or driving cars that denote their specific economic status as they compete with others to reach the next green light.

"Several neighborhoods have posted armed militias at their gates. The homeless are finally being eradicated in a methodical fashion through the use of MR762 rifles that have been distributed to specially trained boys and girls. These are hard times. Fellow citizens, if you intend to survive, you must take the law into your own hands."

"I can hardly wait to get home for a little peace and quiet."

"So many people are out of a job, but yet this lunatic is being paid union wages. It wouldn't be so bad if the bus was actually moving."

"I've already submitted a written complaint about the driver but the transportation agency sent me a pair of orange ear plugs instead of issuing a formal response."

The traffic is finally moving slowly. Gunfire can be heard in the distance. Several large gray Apache double propeller helicopters fly by quickly overhead as they lunge towards the inner city.

"I don't believe in anything anymore. They're always making movies in L.A. I've lived here my entire life and have never seen anyone with a gun. I'm living in the land of the free. I work, pay my taxes, and enjoy life. The secret ballot ensures my right to vote. That's democracy."

"Ignorant people elect stupid people. That's called fascism. If it was all going so great, why are you riding a bus? You need to get your head examined."

A man standing on the street corner puffs on a cigar while laughing at the spectacle of cars, buses, and trucks that are struggling to move along the narrow two-lane passageway. He flicks ashes into his palm.

"They've overtaken Hollywood. The radio is speaking in Spanish."

31

Metro Rail Purple Line Tar Pits Station

"You just missed her. She was incredibly sexy. Completely nude. She was yelling something about the end of the world. She jumped onto the tracks and ran into the tunnel. She couldn't have gotten very far. The train pulled into the station just a moments after she disappeared into the darkness."

"I didn't see her. There were so many people and I've been working on my acceptance speech."

"I've never seen a woman with such a vivacious attitude. I'm no sex maniac but I sure felt like kissing her delicious ass."

"Have you been drinking? I smell cheap whiskey."

I had a double shot, I mean, I held the glass with both hands so as not to spill a drop."

"Maybe you were just seeing things."

"Oh she was real. I almost ran in after her. I've always had a way with the feminine kind."

"It's better not to chase unattainable fantasies."

"Yeah, I could marry a beauty like that."

"That kind of beauty only exists in a decaying mind. Here, be quick, drink this half pint of *mescal*. I've been saving it for someone like you."

"Thanks. Mmmm."

"Now close your eyes. I'll wake you when we get to North Hollywood."

"She was so luscious."

The oval concrete walls of the subway tunnel are illuminated by electric sparks as the train rolls on tracks that lead deeper into the earth. The rumbling and banging of stainless steel wheels on metal tracks is thunderous. White lights flash at various intervals and are interspersed with blue signal lights as the train approaches each station.

"I'd like to see her again. Oh, my love goddess, lost in the black hole."

32

The train car is filled with many people who all appear to be over-worked. Many are slumped over in their seats while others are barely hanging onto the safety bars. The expanse of the human humdrum experience is riding on this subterranean train as riders rub shoulder-to-shoulder in dissociative shrugs of absolute apathy.

"Stand clear, the doors are opening."

The train is evacuated in a silent stampede. I did not notice the drunk-en man leave from the seat next to me as he must have exited through a rear door. I am alone in the rail car as the train moves at high speed through the tunnel. It seems as though time has been revoked. It is difficult to sense how long I have been riding through the cavernous route. I'll get off at the next station but I'm not sure if it will take minutes or years to get there. Flashing blue lights indicate the next station as the train slows to stop.

"Stand clear, the doors are opening."

A crushing flow of people enter the rail car making it impossible to stand up to leave before the doors have closed again. The composi-tion of human beings is distinctly different than the previous group. All of the riders have shed their clothing and are posing provocatively for everyone to see their immodest nude bodies. I am the only rider who is wearing pants, a shirt, and a pair of shoes.

"Go ahead. Take it all off. Strip. We are all equal down here. It's O.K. to have sex with anyone and everyone. No one will object. We all believe in being free with our bodies, you know, *Freikoerperkultur*, Free Body Culture, or FKK. Here, let me loosen your belt."

I made a vow of abstinence for the day and won't allow myself to be touched by anyone. Many of the undulating warm bodies are gro-tesquely misshapen but some are intensely sexually desirable. Some-one has crawled underneath my seat and has been untying my shoe laces. My shirt has disappeared with a slight tug from several strang-ers. Someone is pulling my hair as others lick my back. Mostly every-one is copulating and masturbating in a mass orgy as the train rubs up against the walls producing intense friction in a frenzied detour through an endless chasm that has opened up to reveal a vaguely familiar world. I'm not sure who is fucking whom. I feel as though I have been here many times before. Hands are covering my eyes, my fingers are being bitten, all clothing has been peeled away. The overwhelming scent of sex is intoxicating. The train is melting away.

"Stand clear, the doors are opening."

Washington Boulevard and Soto Street

"Tamales, champurrado, tacos urbanos."

"I'll take a cup of *champurrado*."

"No hablo inglés, señor."

"Here's one dollar."

"Gracias."

The middle-aged couple has set up shop at the back of the bus selling food stuffs on the morning commute. The man plays Mexican folk tunes on the harmonica while the woman handles all cash transactions. A Styrofoam storage box keeps the food warm and a family-sized plastic thermos is used for the hot chocolate-*maíz* drink.

"I wouldn't eat their tacos. Those two are always hanging around the mortuaries on Beverly Boulevard. They're unscrupulous types who shouldn't be handling meat, you know, it could be gang-banger leftovers."

"I'm not hungry."

"Most likely, *tacos de cholos muertos*. You know, the never-ending meat supply that comes by cheaply but yet at too high a price. Urban legends taste best with a bit of *cilantro* and *jalapeño*."

"You certainly don't have much respect for the dead. Gang killings are a serious problem."

"Once you eat human, you'll always want more than what's on the usual menu. They rely on an ancient recipe for the daily special."

"Cannibalism is a great sin."

"Dos tacos de locos para el señor, por favor."

The man is playing a simple song while the woman hums along in a contemporary minimalist counterpoint that is right on key as she pours steaming *orchata* into a white plastic cup. The woman places two tacos on a paper plate.

"Here, you go. Bottom feeders are above the rest."

34

Many riders are eating and drinking as the bus rolls towards the industrial sector. Many riders have purchased several tacos that are contained in plastic bags, possibly for lunch breaks or for dinner.

"Make sure you don't chew on a spent bullet like the time I broke a molar on the hardened lead. Hey, this is my stop. Hope you enjoy your meal. *Ciao*."

I'm sitting alone at a window seat. I've placed the plate atop my outmoded briefcase that contains three ready-to-go Molotov cocktails that are filled with sweet pit bull milk. I'm wearing a 1970's leisure suit, with an oversized shirt, and a wide striped tie. The black wig is parted on the side and is framed by bushy sideburns. My eyebrows are shaved and have been replaced with strips from an unlucky broken mirror.

"If you don't want to eat the tacos, my son would be happy to consume a little extra meat. He's a growing boy."

The overgrown child is scooping out chunks of white fleshy material from a folded corn tortilla. His mother wipes his mouth with the sleeve of her sheer silk blouse.

"He likes the brains, that's what makes him so smart. The teacher says he's almost like a genius."

I've decided to perform an autopsy on the tacos. The tortillas have a tough skin texture and the contents are made up of shredded meat that is mixed with onions, chopped tomatoes, and red salsa. The meat appears to be from the same source as I use a plastic fork to align and match the brown flesh on the plate. I can almost make out several inked letters that seem to spell out a common gang name with several other markings that clearly indicate that the meat comes from the throat and neck area of a man or woman. I also take a look at the drink and notice that unseeing eyeballs are floating on the surface.

"Didn't your parents teach you not to let good food go to waste? You should be slapped across that smug face of yours."

"Be careful that the boy doesn't become a careless carnivore. Instead of licking your sticky fingers, he should eat junk food for breakfast. He shouldn't be hand fed by his mother because Oedipal gluttony could kill his innocence. Sometimes going organic can go too far."

I've placed the tacos into a plastic bag and have put a lid on the cup. I'll ride the bus into Vernon where I'll give the meat a proper burial in an unpaved parking area. I'll light a candle when I get home.

35

Barrington Avenue and Terryhill Place

The side winding avenue is lined with patches of magenta and orange bougainvillea that flourish against the backdrop of modern pastel-colored multi-level apartment complexes. Many people are walking their pampered pet pedigree dogs on designer-label leashes while carrying environmentally-friendly transparent plastic bags of prized superior canine shit. The accelerating bus defies centrifugal forces, ignoring red lights, avoiding collisions with other vehicles, as it sprays a condensation trail of oil and water onto the cracked asphalt. The bus is filled with tightly packed riders, many are standing and clinging to safety bars while those who are sitting desperately grab onto their padded seats. The onboard flat screen monitors display special effected black and white moving images as a smiling male model narrates a scripted version of promotional material that intimates the authority of official news. The amplified voice speaks loudly via hidden built-in speakers.

"Predator drones roam enemy skies spotting insurgents in the mountainous terrain. As you can see through the eyes of a smart bomb, their reign of terror ends with a single blast."

I'm standing near the rear door, sandwiched between domestic workers who have spent the day cleaning, gardening, and performing maintenance work at mansions along the exclusive realm of Mulholland Drive. Several casually dressed European vacationers are clutching their newly acquired gift bags from The Getty Center. A few students read books as they study physics, biology, history, and architecture in the cramped spaces of the vibrating bus.

"Men and women wear striped prison garb while being forced to march under the hot Arizona sun. The sheriff is holding young children at gunpoint until they admit to their crime of illegal border crossing."

An older man and a younger man are banging their pelvises against each other while a middle-aged woman stares intently as she rubs her breasts and hips. The opened ventilation windows allow cool wind to blow turbulently, causing scarves, hair, papers, and debris, to fly and flutter in dispersed patterns of chaotic disarray.

"The wave of the future is here with many convenient medications that can make life easier. Do you feel sudden hostility, lethargy, suicidal thoughts, four-hour long erections, and impossible urges that will never be fulfilled? Liver damage, heart attacks, and other adverse effects shouldn't be taken lightly, but most Americans would agree that everything is better after being injected with our patented serum."

I'm wearing a knee-length black wool coat and black boots. A black silk scarf is wrapped over my hair and tied neatly under my chin while tucked under the buttoned-down collar. My face is visible with bright red rouge highlighting my cheekbones and mint green mascara augments the effects of 1-inch long false eyelashes. I have not spoken to anyone in nearly a week. I have not touched or been touched by anyone in more than a year. I am holding the metal safety rails and have been looking at the faded spectrum of successive apartments that pass inconsequentially beyond memory. The bus is moving faster as all of the riders sway from left to right.

"Older son or daughter living at home? Can't get them to do their fair share? We've got the best solution to clear out your nest. Call your recruiter any time of day or night. We do pick ups 24-7."

The evening sun is nearing the horizon as it is being devoured by the moon's silhouette during a partial eclipse. The image burns into my retina triggering overpowering primal fears, releasing adrenaline followed by the immediate withdrawal effects of startled shaking and coldness within the core of my body. I feel a direct connection to the sun despite the many millions of miles that separate it from me as I ride on a planet that rotates, tilts, orbits, and drifts further out into space while I'm aboard a bus that can barely remain on the earth's surface.

"The economy depends on your stimulating support. Shop until it hurts. Spend what you don't have so that you can possess everything that your heart desires. Swipe away dull passions by using your debit and credit cards to renew your happiness. Overdraft charges and late payment fees may apply."

The coldness has spread out from my bone marrow to the muscles, the skin, and onto the outer edges of black clothing. Frost patches are weighing down on the false eyelashes simultaneously producing a frigid and sultry allure. The freezing wind is solidifying some hapless riders in place while others have already been sealed in thick layers of blue glacial ice. Chattering teeth and panting foggy breaths are echoing a lament of social paralysis that reverberates against the brittle human forms.

"You still have time to accept our free offer. Call us now and you'll receive additional items at no cost. We want you to be a repeat customer. All you have to do is sign our extended agreement. Don't think, just do."

The speeding bus chases embittered shadows in the twilight of consciousness as my eyelashes crash down on all traces of light.

37

10 Freeway and 110 Freeway

Cómo reportar vandalismo de manera segura y anonima.

How to report vandalism safely and anonymously.

Note la descripción del vándalo.

Note description of vandal.

Observe el número al frente de autobús.

Observe bus number posted at front of bus.

Fijese en la hora.

Check the time.

Llame cuando esté fuera de peligro.

Call when safely away from danger.

Llama al:

Call:

1-888-950-1233

The English and Spanish language anti-vandalism posters are aligned side by side above the front row seats of the bus. The simple graphics show a boy making a squiggle mark on a bus window while a generic unisex figure calls the authorities on a mobile phone.

"Mind if I sit next to you? The man at the rear of the bus is masturbating and I'm simply not interested in looking at him. He does the same thing each afternoon on the way home from work. He holds the newspaper over his lap and no one else ever seems to notice his filthy behavior."

"He looks like he's asleep, but his hand is underneath the newspaper."

"My ex-husband was always touching himself and it always made me want to puke. I never once put my lips to that thing."

"He's snoring and drooling."

"Disgusting. He's laughing to himself."

"He's unconscious."

"I can't understand why men have to put their hands on themselves or on anything that moves. I've never let a man touch my vagina until he's proven his worth."

"No exceptions?"

"Never."

The woman and I continue to converse as we ride for several miles while the bus moves at a slow pace along with several thousand vehicles in the afternoon traffic jam. The mountains, Hollywood hills, downtown skyline, palm trees, flying birds, and much of the city can all be seen moving in relation to their distance from the bus as translucent clouds of tinted pollutants are blown towards the sea. The woman is smartly dressed and probably works in a high rise building.

"And that is the last time I'll ever let a man fuck me that way because it's so unnatural. Oh, what am I telling you for? You've probably heard it, seen it, and done it all before."

"Emotional scars and laugh lines are all etched on my face. Yes, I've played many games, only to win and lose a few trophies."

"All it takes is a slight miscalculation in judging a man's character, or even an enticing brash act of machismo, to catch me off guard. I'm extremely intelligent and a good-hearted human being. My sexual activity usually involves mercy fucks. I've been married five times."

The man has removed the newspaper from his lap, momentarily exposing his flaccid penis. He lifts himself up in his seat and zips his pants. His right hand is glistening.

"I told you, he's an absolute monster."

"Yeah, he sure can fool the public eye."

"He's my boss. Don't tell anyone."

Using his wet forefinger, the man scrawls a block letter message on the Plexiglas window:

CALL: 1-888-950-1233

39

Metro Rail Blue Line Del Amo Station

Eighty thousand riders make their daily commute on the 22-mile long light rail Metro Rail Blue Line, allowing them to momentarily escape deeply impoverished urban regions in an attempt to reach the critical social and economic juncture of downtown Los Angeles, where the possibility of elevated lifestyle options might arise. By the end of each day, most riders return empty-handed to their blighted neighborhoods with a dim hope of revisiting the city in grand style. Vast stretches of the Metro Blue Line thoroughfare are unsecured by partial barriers that fail to prevent children from playing on the visible tracks that serve as a viable spatial alternative to city and county parks where random and wanton violence often occur. At certain points, where tracks meet street crossings, it is easy to imagine how some deluded drivers might decide to bypass unconvincing warning signs and lowered wooden gates, and then, without hesitation, propel themselves forward onto the tracks without truly believing that they would be instantly killed by a moving train that weighs many tons. During its two decades of operation, nearly a hundred pedestrians and motorists have been killed, making it the deadliest active urban rail line in the United States.

"Wow, I was nearly stabbed by hoodlums on the station platform. Those punks wanted to steal my prosthetic arm. I cut one of them pretty bad. Shit, what fun."

"Keep it to yourself. There's no pity in this city."

"It's a contravention of my human rights and that's why I pushed the other motherfucker onto the tracks. I left the bad arm in Vietnam because this is the one that got me back. I'm one badass *veterano*."

"Where did you leave your bad eye?"

"My brother took it out during my mother's funeral because he thought I was chasing his lady. Mama always told me not to wink."

"Not much left of you to cry about."

"Man, I've shed a million tears for my past miserable life but now I'm always having a good time. I'm a lucky man. I can come and go as I please. Everyone can tease. But it's me who's gonna seize them by the throat. I'm a trained killer but spend my days spreading love to all the beautiful people because I'm true to my word."

"Tears and words evaporate easily.

40

"Dust to dust before you know it."

A young woman rushes through the crowd followed by two casually dressed men who have drawn semi-automatic pistols that are trained on their targets. The police badges reflect distorted images of the feck-less faces of many riders who remain unmoved by the commotion. The woman fires several rounds hitting two women in the head and chest. The two men shoot a single man nearly thirty times in the torso.

"Subjects down. The package has been neutralized."

The woman uses the mobile phone to video-document the carnage. One man holds the two dead women up by their hair while the other lifts the dead man's head so that his motionless face smiles for the camera.

"Any of you fucks think about complaining got another thing coming. These terrorists almost got away with killing everyone on the train. Now, go about your business. You can switch cars at the next stop or you can stay to get a close look at exterminated vermin."

The train slows down.

"Stand clear, the doors are opening."

The police officers exit quickly along with the large crowd, leaving only several riders, and three corpses that appear to be floating in a single pool of blood.

"Stand clear, the doors are closing."

"That's just what I didn't need. Flashbacks are a bitch."

"I almost talked with the first woman who was hit because I wanted to get her phone number. They would have shot me for conspiring with a pretty terrorist."

"License to kill. In my day they called it pacification."

"I've had too many close calls. I'm down to my last cat life."

"I believe in reincarnation. I'll come back as venomous *coloti*. My sting was deadly in the 70's and will be even more fearsome in the next life.

"So, you lost your mind in Trang Bang? You killed too many."

"All I've got left is my love and affection for the sweetness of life."

41

Colorado Street Bridge

"We're headed in the wrong direction. The arroyo used to be over there and the mountains never used to block the view of the desert. We're really high up. Stop the bus. I want to jump off."

"Me too, I want to jump."

"Suicide bridge is what it is. Every time I cross I want to jump too."

"Driver, make a quick right and we'll all go over the bridge with you."

"No. Whatever you do, don't look down."

The bus slows and rolls to a smooth stop on the center yellow double line, halfway across the bridge. The front and back doors open. The engine shuts down as the driver gets up from his seat and alights from the bus. He walks from the middle of the street and steps onto the sidewalk. He lights a cigarette as he talks into a mobile phone. He's laughing as he removes his watch, and empties his pockets of coins, keys, and his wallet. He places all of the items into a neat pile on the curb. He takes a long drag on the cigarette. The driver goes to the row of interlocking vertical decorative wrought iron bars that serve as a suicide barrier. He continues his conversation on the phone as he scales the bars quickly to fall off the bridge, and vanishes into the abyss of the Arroyo Seco.

"Now what are we supposed to do?"

"Let's play follow the leader."

"Yeah, fuck it."

"Je m'ennuie."

Fifteen riders, some elderly, but mostly young, along with three small children, exit the bus and go to the suicide barrier. The children are easily tossed over the edge without a sound and the elderly are lifted and pushed past the point of no return. The rest manage to go over the side of the bridge without any difficulty.

"I can't believe what I'm seeing. Has the world gone mad?"

"It's mass suicide. I'll look silly if I stay here. They all looked so happy and I'm so unhappy."

42

Three more riders run from the bus towards the suicide barrier and jump over it in a spontaneous display of acrobatic twirls and back flips.

"Mass hypnosis. Mass hysteria. Self-annihilation just ain't my thing."

A young woman repeatedly bangs her head on the windshield.

"Nada vale nada."

A large man falls to his knees with outstretched arms.

"Every last one of you, listen to me. What I'm about to do is of my own free will. I've never followed the herd. But what we have here is an inspired flock that flies into the face of destiny. I bid you all, farewell."

The man bows and kisses a selected few riders on the lips. He removes his coat, shirt, tie, and undershirt. He takes a penknife and carves a message into his chest and abdomen:

EVERY BIRD MUST FALL

The man smiles slyly as he exits the bus. He takes a running leap over the edge of the bridge.

"Did you see that? He must have been as light as a feather."

"Zelfmoord. **Self death**. *Suicidio*. There isn't much to taking a faithless leap into nothingness."

Less than ten riders remain on the bus. We all sit silently for more than an hour. The sound of fast blowing wind intermixes with the noise produced from speeding traffic on the adjacent 210 freeway. Eventually, news helicopters appear in the sky. Several police vehicles pull alongside the bus. One officer attempts to climb over the suicide barrier but is beaten down with metal flashlights by his own team, then handcuffed, and put into the back seat of a police cruiser. A new driver nonchalantly boards the bus, starts the engine, and sets the bus in motion, first slowly, then picks up enough speed to nearly send us all over the edge. We move faster and farther away from the bridge.

"Fucking conformists. I'm glad they all jumped. Our society needs people with a sense of purpose."

"Take me back, I forgot to jump."

"People like you weaken the species."

43

Angels Flight

"We're in free-fall. It's the only funicular in the world that operates without established safety features. It's a much better ride than what any of the regional amusement parks have to offer."

"I agree. We'll definitely be involved in a horrific crash in a few moments."

"The politically-greased track is less than 300 feet long on a 33% grade. Add gravity, momentum, inoperable brakes, faulty haulage system, and a phantom operator, to give us the ride of a lifetime."

"It's a relic of the past that has outlived its usefulness."

"It's a historic national treasure."

"By any other name it is still a deathtrap."

"When I was a kid, I often boarded Angels Flight on 3rd Street and Hill Street. It cost a nickle to ride and it was a great way to reach the top of Bunker Hill. I never thought that I'd be riding it for the last time a half block south from its point of origin."

"Well, you can't beat the view."

"I need more time to get everything in order. I've started reading a book without a title. I know that I'm supposed to be doing a few more activities but can't remember them all at once. Everything seems to have gone by too quickly."

"It's all an illusion. You've never gotten around to completing any truly important tasks. Everything has always been left undone. So, in a way, it doesn't matter. At least you'll have the satisfaction of knowing that your mark on earth will be easily erased."

"I'm not dead yet."

"You certainly don't seem to be very concerned over my fate. We're in this predicament together."

"There has to be a way out of this without having to resort to desperate measures."

"There's no escaping obvious conclusions."

44

"I've done everything to outdistance myself from anything that is inherently obvious."

"You'll be a common corpse with no distinguishable marks in a matter of seconds."

"Impossible. The upcoming collision will be survivable. Only one of us will die."

"You're in no position to argue about the fact that we're headed straight for our doom."

"You're wrong. Nothing makes sense. The funicular ceased operation at the start of the 21st Century. And I'm not certain who you might be. I don't know your name. This isn't a dream or a hallucination. It's all too bitterly real."

"Pinch me."

"But we're moving in slow motion while talking at normal speed. The laws of physics are being violated here. It could be a philosophical or perceptual chasm."

"Actually we're moving at a high rate of speed and running out of precious time for any of your excuses to be invoked here. You say that you don't recognize me but you know perfectly well who I am."

"Redundancy, duplicity, elasticity."

"You've always travelled backwards and forwards in an endless loop of self-denial."

"The crash will probably involve lots of pain."

"You're already beginning to stink."

"I'm afraid."

"You should laugh loudly. It's a much better exit than cowardly cries of anguish."

"When I first got on, it never occurred to me that I'd be riding so fast for only such a short distance. I paid full fare. I want my money back. It feels like I never went anywhere."

"Ready now, here it is, the inevitable dead-end."

45

Harry Gamboa Jr.

Since 1972, Harry Gamboa Jr. has been actively creating works in various media that document and interpret the contemporary urban Chicano experience.

He was a co-founder of Asco (Spanish for nausea) 1972-1987, the East L.A. conceptual-performance art group.

His work has been exhibited nationally and internationally: Musée de l'Elysée, Lausanne, Switzerland (2009); Los Angeles County Museum of Art (2008, 2001); Museo Tamayo Arte Contemporaneo, Mexico City (2006); Centre Pompidou, Paris (2006); 1995 Biennial, Whitney Museum of American Art.

His work has been featured in numerous publications: *Los Angeles Times*; *The New York Times*; *Reforma* (Mexico City); *Artforum*; *Art in America*; *Frieze* (London); *The Wall Street Journal*; *The Journal of American Drama and Theatre*.

He is the author of:
Urban Exile: Collected Writings of Harry Gamboa Jr.
(ed. Chon A. Noriega)
University of Minnesota Press
1998
ISBN 0-8166-3052-6 paper
ISBN 0-8166-3051-8 cloth

CPSIA information can be obtained
at www.ICGtesting.com
Printed in the USA
LVHW061557160122
708712LV00005B/60

9 781448 670307